THE COMICS IN THIS BOOK WERE ORIGINALLY PUBLISHED IN

THE PHOENIX

AN AMAZING WEEKLY COMIC WITH
BRAND NEW JAMIE SMART COMICS
& THRILLING SERIALISED ADVENTURES
DELIVERED TO YOUR DOOR EVERY WEEK

BE THE FIRST TO READ ALL-NEW
EPISODES OF BUNNY VS MONKEY!

www.thephoenixcomic.co.uk

Adaptation, additional artwork and colours by Sammy Borras.
Cover design by Paul Duffield and Jamie Smart.

Bunny vs Monkey: Bunny Bonanza is a
DAVID FICKLING BOOK

Book 9 in the Bunny vs Monkey series, available from thephoenixcomic.shop and all good bookstores:

First published in Great Britain in 2024 by
David Fickling Books, 31 Beaumont Street, Oxford, OX1 2NP

Text and illustrations © Fumboo Ltd, 2024

978-1-78845-306-6
1 3 5 7 9 10 8 6 4 2

The right of Jamie Smart to be identified as the author and illustrator of this work
has been asserted in accordance with the Copyright, Designs and Patents Act 1988.

MIX
Paper from
responsible sources
FSC® C104723

DAVID FICKLING BOOKS Reg. No. 8340307
A CIP catalogue record for this book is available from the British Library.
Printed and bound in China by Toppan Leefung.

JAMIE SMART'S

BUNNY VS MONKEY

BUNNY BONANZA!

"BUNNYLESS"

A NEW YEAR DAWNS UPON THE WOODS...

...THE ANIMALS ARE ENJOYING THE SNOW...

PAF!!

...THE ROBOTS ARE PREPARING FOR SPRING...

ZZZT!

BZZT!!

...AND MONKEY IS...

NYAHHHHH!

...BEING MONKEY.

IN FACT, EVERYTHING IS EXACTLY AS IT SHOULD BE...

...EVERYTHING EXCEPT A SMALL HOUSE IN THE MIDDLE OF THE WOODS...

A SMALL...

...EMPTY...

...HOUSE.

SIGH.

CREAK!

BUNNY?

DID YOU COME HOME YET?

OH DEAR, YOU DIDN'T EVEN FINISH YOUR TEA.

SOB!

I DON'T THINK BUNNY IS COMING BACK.

I FEEL LIKE IT'S MY FAULT.

I FEEL SO GUILTY.

IT WAS HIS CHOICE.

BUNNY IS **FINE.**

8

OH, FINE, IT **IS** A ROBOT BUNNY.

WE THOUGHT YOU'D BE HAPPY!

FZZP!
BPPT!

YOU'VE ALL BEEN WHINING ABOUT HOW BUNNY'S GONE, SO SKUNKY BUILT YOU A **NEW** BUNNY.

IT'S, UH... A PROTOTYPE.

I'VE SPENT THE LAST FEW WEEKS TRYING TO RUIN ALL YOUR LIVES, BUT YOU'VE BEEN SO BUSY MISSING BUNNY YOU HAVEN'T EVEN **NOTICED!!**

HUFF!

LIKE WEENIE'S HOUSE, FOR EXAMPLE. I FILLED THAT WITH **JELLY.**

OH, THAT WAS YOU?

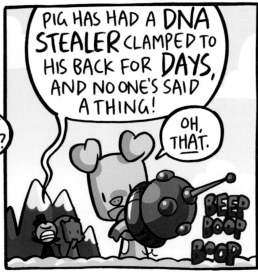

PIG HAS HAD A **DNA STEALER** CLAMPED TO HIS BACK FOR **DAYS,** AND NO ONE'S SAID A THING!

OH, THAT.

BEEP DOOP BEEP

ALLOW ME, **LE FOX**, TO EXPLAIN. WITH ZE BUNNY GONE, I THOUGHT ZAT IT MIGHT HELP FOR US TO ALL **SWITCH ROLES**.

ZAT WAY, WE COULD FIND A **NEW** BUNNY!

AI COULD BE BUNNY!

I DON'T **WANT** TO BE BUNNY.

OOOOH, SHE DOES **SOUND** LIKE BUNNY.

YOU'VE ALL GONE **CRAZY!**

NOT ME. I'M HAVING FAR MORE FUN BEING **SKUNKY!**

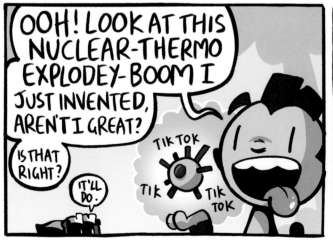

OOH! LOOK AT THIS **NUCLEAR-THERMO EXPLODEY-BOOM** I JUST INVENTED, AREN'T I GREAT?

IS THAT RIGHT?

IT'LL DO.

TIK TOK
TIK
TIK TOK

BUT WAIT, IF YOU'RE BEING SKUNKY, THEN WHO'S BEING **MONKEY?**

PLLP!

15

"STICKLEPLOPS"

HANG ON, I THOUGHT BUNNY FLOATED UP INTO THE CLOUDS OR SOMETHING. SO HOW COME HE'S RIGHT THERE?

I HAVE A THEORY ABOUT THAT.

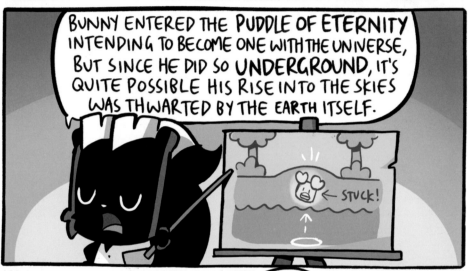

BUNNY ENTERED THE PUDDLE OF ETERNITY INTENDING TO BECOME ONE WITH THE UNIVERSE, BUT SINCE HE DID SO UNDERGROUND, IT'S QUITE POSSIBLE HIS RISE INTO THE SKIES WAS THWARTED BY THE EARTH ITSELF.

← STUCK!

PUT SIMPLY, I BELIEVE BUNNY HAS BEEN IMPRISONED IN THE GROUND.

THAT IS, UNTIL WE SET HIM FREE!

LOOK. THIS IS A VERY NICE HOUSE, BUT I JUST DON'T REMEMBER ANYTHING IN IT!

PLOOM!

SHRIEK!

THESE ARE MY **STICKLE-PLOPS!**

THEY'RE DESIGNED TO STICK TO **ANYTHING!**

MONKEY, WHAT HAVE YOU **DONE?!**

I'VE IMPROVED THIS PLACE CONSIDERABLY IS WHAT I'VE DONE!

COME TO ME, MY STICKLEPLOP CHILDREN! LET US TAKE OVER THE WOODS **TOGETHER!**

UMM...

YOU MIGHT ALL WANT TO COME INSIDE.

28

"FLYING FUN"

MEET **F1-5H**, THE GENETICALLY ENGINEERED TANK DRIVER!

FISH HAVE A REMARKABLE SENSE OF DIRECTION, YOU KNOW.

WITH F1-5H PSYCHICALLY CONTROLLING THE TANK, WE CAN AIM IT TOWARDS WHATEVER WE CHOOSE!

AND WHAT ARE YOU AIMING IT AT?

YOUR **HOUSE!**

HA HA HAA!

JUST AS A TEST RUN, YOU UNDERSTAND.

WHAT? NO! I'M JUST GETTING USED TO THAT HOUSE!

THERE'S ONLY ONE DESIGN FLAW I'VE DISCOVERED SO FAR.

OF ALL THE FISH I COULD HAVE CHOSEN FOR THE F1-5H...

CLOMP CLOMP CLOMP!

...I CHOSE A **FLYING FISH!**

NYAH!

HUP!

GAH!

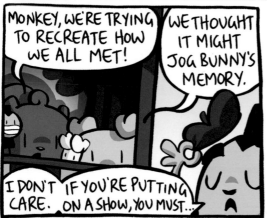

36

38

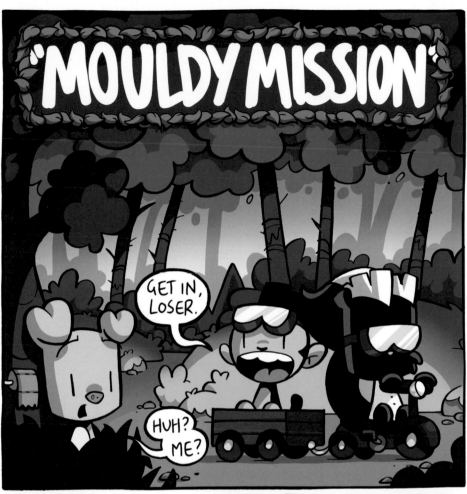

40

THERE IT IS! THE STINKIEST, GROSSEST, MOST MOULDY BOTTLE OF MILK IN EXISTENCE!

YOU JUST HAVE TO GO THROUGH THE **COWS** TO GET TO IT!

ULP!

I GOT IT! HURGHH!

WHAT ARE YOU GOING TO DO WITH IT?

PIG THIS MILK, THIS **DISGUSTING** MILK, CONTAINS THE **PERFECT DNA** FOR MY MOST EXTRAORDINARY SCHEME **EVER!**

SLOP!

ARGH!

EURGH!
OH, THAT'S
HORRIBLE.

OH.
OH NO.
IT SMELLS.

"A MOMENT OF CALM"

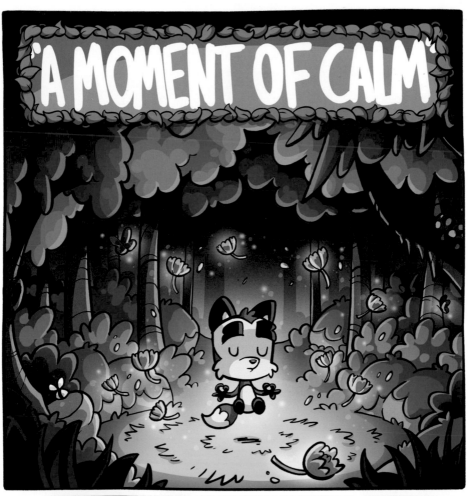

HEY, LE FOX!

HMPH.

WHAT?

PLOMP!

YOU'RE AN ALL-KNOWING CREATURE OF THE WOODS, RIGHT? YOUR ENTIRE BEING IS PERFECTLY ATTUNED TO THE WORLD AROUND YOU?

OUI.

WELL THEN, MAYBE YOU CAN TELL ME...

...WHERE MY SOCKS ARE?

SOCKS? YOU ARE A MONKEY! YOU DON'T **WEAR** SOCKS!

I DO, AND I'VE LOST THEM.

LEAVE ME ALONE, YOU IDIOT. I MUST RETURN TO BEING AT ONE WITH THE UNIVERSE.

LE FOX! HAVE YOU SEEN OUR PET WORM, PETER?

WE'VE LOST HIM!

GAH!

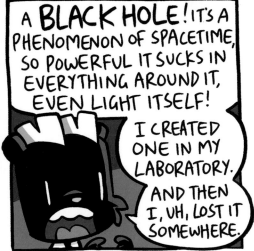

52

53

"THE CAVE"

OH NO! HMS PANCAKES HAS SAILED INTO THE UNKNOWN!!

HMS PANCAKES

55

57

60

BUNNY! GIVE US BACK THAT BIN!

H - E - L - P
M - E

REMARKABLE! IT'S LEARNING LANGUAGE!

WHAT, EXACTLY, ARE YOU PLANNING TO DO WITH THIS BIN?

WELL, STUDY IT OF COURSE! MAYBE CUT BITS OFF AND PUT THEM UP OUR NOSES.

YAY!

THEN **NO**. THIS BIN IS A LIVING CREATURE, AND IT DESERVES THE SAME RIGHTS AS **WE** DO.

THE RIGHT TO BE ZAPPED WITH LASERS?

WELL, YES, I SUPPOSE THAT DOES HAPPEN TO US SOMETIMES...

63

"BIRTHDAY WISHES!"

71

73

"THE DAY THE SKY FELL IN!" (PART ONE)

EVERYONE! GET TO THE SAFETY OF BUNNY'S HOUSE!

WHAT?

WHY?

DON'T ARGUE! JUST GET INSIDE! IN! IN!!

SHRIEK!

GIBBER!

THAT'S NOT IMPORTANT. WHAT MATTERS IS WE'RE ALL IN THE SAFEST PLACE POSSIBLE!

MY HOUSE?

SKUNKY, MY HOUSE IS VERY NICE, BUT IT WON'T SURVIVE THE **MOON** CRASHING INTO IT!

YEAH IT WILL...

Boop!

...EVER SINCE I INSTALLED THIS **FORCE FIELD** AROUND IT!

SW OP!

OOOOOOOOOOOH!

WHY... WHY DID YOU DO THAT?

DUNNO.

MOON.

SQUEEZE

IT'S NOT HOLDING!

NOT TO WORRY!

BOOP!

I ALSO INSTALLED **MECHANICAL CHICKEN LEGS!!**

ALL WE CAN DO IS STAY IN HERE AND WATCH EARTH'S IMPENDING DOOM!

WHAT? NO!

SKUNKY, YOU MUST HAVE INSTALLED SOMETHING IN THIS HOUSE WHICH MIGHT ACTUALLY BE OF USE!

BOOP!

WELL...

HOT DOG

HOT DOG VENDING MACHINE!

WE'RE SAVED!

UM. HELLO?

MUNCH MUNCH!

80

84

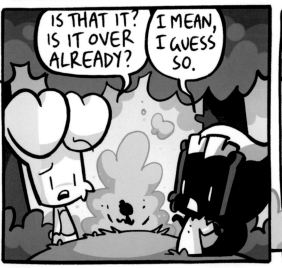

97

98

"HIDDEN LOOT"

QUITE A FEW YEARS AGO...

ARR! ARR! ARR! ARR! ARR! ARR!

WE MADE IT, CAP'N REDBEARD! WE SAILED THE SEVEN SEAS AND FOUND THE MOST REMOTE STRETCH OF BEACH ON THE PLANET.

AYE, THAT WE DID, BOATSWAIN.

JUST THE RIGHT SPOT TO BURY ALL ME **TREASURE.**

AND, OF COURSE, THIS **MYSTERIOUS GEM** I DISCOVERED ON ME TRAVELS.

WHAT DOES IT DO, CAP'N?

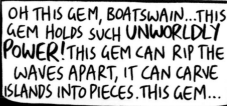

OH THIS GEM, BOATSWAIN...THIS GEM HOLDS SUCH **UNWORLDLY POWER!** THIS GEM CAN RIP THE WAVES APART, IT CAN CARVE ISLANDS INTO PIECES. THIS GEM...

FRRPP!

GASP...THE GEM MAKES YOU **FART?!**

I THOUGHT IT MIGHT BE FOUR MONTHS OF EATING NOTHING BUT ROTTEN SAUERKRAUT BUT NO...

...PERHAPS THE GEM CAUSED IT!

IT'S MORE POWERFUL THAN I THOUGHT! WE MUST BURY THIS GEM SO NO ONE WILL FIND IT...

...IN THE WRONG HANDS, IT WOULD BE A CATASTROPHE!

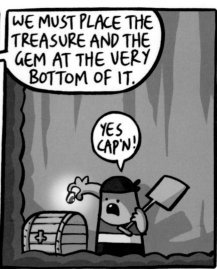

107

"SHUSH!"

IT IS MOI, LE FOX! I FOUND ONE OF SKUNKY'S OLD INVENTIONS, THE NATTER HAMSTER, AND TWEAKED ITS VOICEBOX...

...NOW IT IS A SHUT-UP-A-LUMP!

BUT...BUT WHY?

BECAUSE EVERYONE IN THESE WOODS IS FAR TOO NOISY. IT'S ALL BANG AND WOOSH AND ARGHH, AND IT'S INTERRUPTING MY DAYTIME NAP!

I WAS ONLY SWEEPING.

WELL IT IS TOO LOUD. SILENCE. S'IL VOUS PLAIT.

ZAT IS BETTER ALREADY. AWAY, SHUT-UP-A-LUMP!

WEENIE, I FOUND A ROCK AND PAINTED A FACE ON IT. WOULD YOU LIKE TO SAY HELLO?

I...GUESS?

111

‡HICCUP!‡

WILL YOU BE QUIET?!

WE CAN'T LET LE FOX CARRY ON LIKE THIS. HE'S MAKING LIFE MISERABLE FOR US ALL!

THERE IS SOMEONE WHO COULD HELP US.

YOU... YOU DON'T MEAN..

COR, THANKS FOR MY NEW TRUMPET, GUYS. FOUR HOURS OF LOUD PRACTICE BEGINS...

113

116

NOT REALLY, THESE ARE ALL JUST A BIT... RANDOM.

WELL, BLAME SKUNKY! HE'S NOT INVENTED ANYTHING DECENT IN WEEKS!

THIS IS THE LAST THING!

130

131

USING THE MOST PEACEFULLY QUIET TOILET IN THE WOODS.

OR IT WAS UNTIL YOU TURNED UP!

I AM VERY SORRY TO HAVE INTERRUPTED YOU, MONKEY. I WAS TRYING TO DISCOVER WHAT HOLDS THE GROUND UP.

UMM...

METAL EVE, IT MAY SURPRISE YOU TO LEARN I'M NOT A SCIENTIST, BUT AS FAR AS I UNDERSTAND IT THE GROUND IS HELD UP BY ALL THIS ROCK!

YES, BUT WHAT HOLDS THE ROCK UP?

UMM... MORE ROCK?

WELL WHAT HOLDS THAT ROCK UP?

I DECIDED TO FIND OUT.

THEN COUNT ME IN TOO! LET'S GO LOOKING!

UMM, WHY DO YOU BRING A PICKAXE TO THE TOILET?

BEST NOT TO ASK.

140

145

146

EWW! NOW IT'S ON ME TOO!

HE'S DONE IT. MONKEY'S FINALLY DONE IT...

HE'S DISCOVERED THE PERFECT WAY TO TAKE OVER THE WOODS! NOW NONE OF US WANT TO GET ANYWHERE NEAR HIM!

SQUELCH!

IF I MIGHT SUGGEST... NOW MONKEY IS A CREATURE OF PURE UNTOUCHABLE CHAOS...PERHAPS THE VOICE OF **LOGIC** MIGHT OFFER ZE SOLUTION.

YOU?

NON!. NOT ME...

YOUR PANIC IS MISPLACED. ALL DIRT CAN BE REMOVED WITH THE DAB OF A LICKED TISSUE.

LICK!

DAB DAB!

GASP!

IT WORKS!

LICK MORE TISSUES!!

A LOT OF LICKY DABBING LATER...

YOU ARE SUCH A FILTHY MONKEY!

GRAARG! ARGH! FLIP!

HOW DID YOU GET SO MUCKY?

PFFT! AS IF YOU COULD STOP HIM.

I HAVE TO TRY!

BEEP! BOOP!

THIS ARMOUR MUST DO SOMETHING ELSE.

BOOM!

HUH. WELL, IT SELF-DESTRUCTS.

FLUMP!

STILL, I'VE MANAGED TO APPREHEND THE SUBJECT. QUICKLY, KID, WHAT'S THE FASTEST ROUTE BACK TO THE WOODS?

...SIGH!

BACK IN THE WOODS...

THAT'S ANOTHER VICTORY FOR BUNNY LAW!

BAH!

153

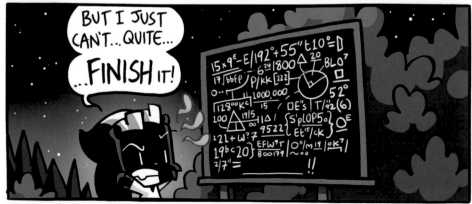

OOH! A PEANUT!

METAL EVE, YOU'RE THE MOST POWERFUL COMPUTER ON THE WHOLE PLANET!

HUP!

YOU MUST BE ABLE TO SOLVE THIS EQUATION!

I CAN'T SOLVE THIS.

WHY EVER NOT?

YOU APPEAR TO HAVE WRITTEN IT UPSIDE DOWN.

THAT'S BETTER. HMM...IS THE ANSWER NINETY HUNDRED AND TWELVE?

HOW...HOW DID YOU DO THAT?

I GUESSED!

157

"BIG BUNNY"

HELLOOOOOOOO?

BUNNNYYYY?

BUNNY'S DISAPPEARED AGAIN!

MAYBE HE WENT SNOWBOARDING.

PIG, THAT'S RIDICULOUS.

IF BUNNY IS ANYWHERE...

...LE FOX WILL KNOW!!

SIGH.

LE FOX WILL KNOW WHAT?

163

'SQUEAK-OOOOO'

SKUNKY! I HAVE MADE A **DECISION.**

I'M GOING TO TAKE OVER THE WOODS, AND CALL IT **MONKEYOPIA!**

UMM...

...HASN'T THAT **ALWAYS** BEEN YOUR PLAN?

I THOUGHT SO TOO. BUT I HAVEN'T DONE IT YET.

WEIRD THAT, ISN'T IT?

OH, HANG ON, THIS IS GOING TO BE MY FAULT, ISN'T IT?

WELL MAYBE IF YOU'D ACTUALLY INVENTED SOMETHING TO HELP ME I'D HAVE DONE IT BY NOW!

SIGH. KNEW IT.

SPIT

166

167

"FISTS OF FUN"

OH! I NEARLY FORGOT TO SHOW YOU!

...THE IRON FISTS!

THE IRON FISTS ARE PLUGGED DIRECTLY INTO THE MAP, GIVING YOU FULL 360° CONTROL!

I DON'T KNOW WHAT THAT MEANS!

WELL, WHY DON'T I SHOW YOU.

171

173

BUNNY! AS YOUR FUTURE RULER, I AM GENEROUSLY OFFERING YOU YOUR PRESENT NOW BEFORE CHAINS AND MANACLES PREVENT YOU FROM FULLY ENJOYING IT!

TAA-DAAAAA!

WHAT... WHAT IS IT?

I'LL SHOW YOU...

...IT'S ACTION BEAVER. FOR ONE DAY ONLY, HE'S ON YOUR SIDE!

RIP! RIP! RIP!

BUT...BUT WE DON'T WANT HIM.

TOO LATE! HE'S YOURS NOW!

TEE HEE HEE!

175

I KNOW YOU'RE ALL TRYING YOUR BEST BUT THIS DOESN'T FEEL LIKE MY BIRTHDAY.

EVERYTHING'S SLIGHTLY OUT OF PLACE.

ESPECIALLY ACTION BEAVER. USUALLY HE'S ALL BEEPING AND FARTING BUT HE HASN'T MADE A SINGLE NOISE SINCE HE'S BEEN HERE!

MAYBE HIS MOUTH IS FULL!

HEE HEE!

FULL? WITH WHAT?

OH BOTHER.

TNT

BOOM!

THAT IS, UNTIL I HEARD ACTION BEAVER, MONKEY, AND SOMETHING THEY CALLED A... NUCLEAR THERMO EXPLODEY BOOM!

THE EXPLOSION WAS SO IMMENSE...

BOOM

...IT BURIED ME IN THE GROUND!

AND EVEN WORSE...

...IT TOTALLY WIPED MY MEMORY!

BUT IF YOU'RE A DIFFERENT BUNNY...

...THEN WHERE'S OUR BUNNY?

I'LL SHOW YOU!

PLONK!

FLIP!

I HAVE BEEN COLLATING ALL ZESE OTHER BUNNIES, AND MAPPING ZEM ALL ACROSS THE WOODS!

AND THEN GIVING ZEM FUNNY NAMES.

ZE ONE WE LOST, ZAT'S NOT BUNNY...

THEN ZERE WAS OLD BUNNY...

ZIS ONE I CALL NEANDER-BUNNY...

YOU THOUGHT BUNNY LAW WAS NOT BUNNY, BUT HE WAS NOT NOT BUNNY.

OH, AND BUNNY LAW MET SARCASTIC BUNNY IN ZE REALM OF ZE HUMANS...

ZERE IS, HOWEVER, ONE BUNNY WHO REMAINS A MYSTERY TO ME...

185

IT'S NOT EASY COMING UP WITH NEW INVENTIONS EVERY WEEK, Y'KNOW.

IT TAKES TIME.

PATIENCE.

AND BESIDES, I SENT METAL STEVE AND ACTION BEAVER OUT TO FIND SOME IDEAS FOR ME..

CRUMP!

NYAH!

SLURRRP

WELLLL? WHAT HAVE YOU BROUGHT BACK?

A HALF-EATEN LEMON PUFF, AN OLD SOCK, AND A CATERPILLAR.

HMM. I'M NOT SURE THERE'S MUCH I CAN INVENT WITH THIS...

ACTION BEAVER FOUND GOLD!

MRRG!

GASP! THE LOST TREASURE OF CAP'N REDBEARD!

191

192

202

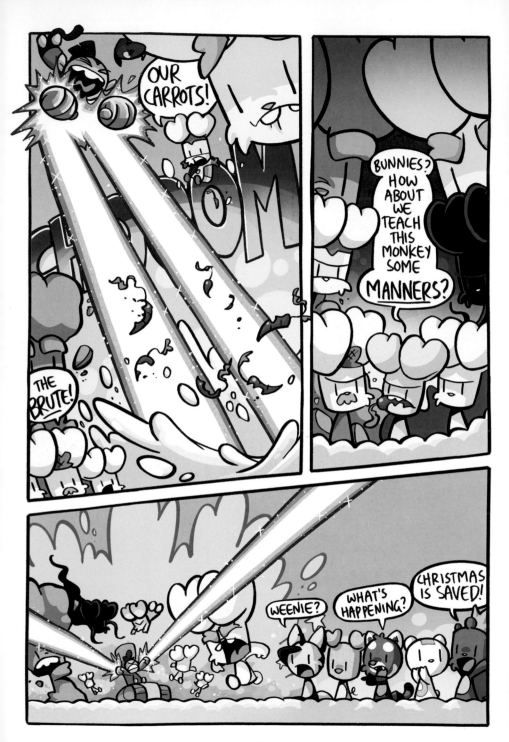

205

HOW TO DRAW SHADOW BUNNY

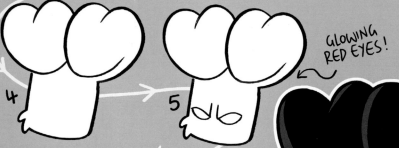

1

BULGING SQUARE!

2

3

TWO EARS!

4

5

GLOWING RED EYES!

BODY IS BLACK GOO!

IT CAN TAKE ANY SHAPE!

6

ADD WEIRD TENTACLES!

7

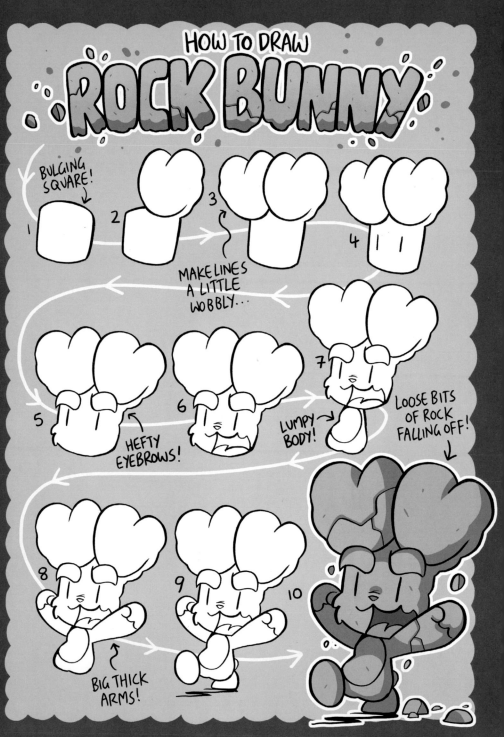

HOW TO DRAW
ROCK BUNNY

BULGING SQUARE!

1

2

3 MAKE LINES A LITTLE WOBBLY...

4

5 HEFTY EYEBROWS!

6

7

LUMPY BODY!

LOOSE BITS OF ROCK FALLING OFF!

8 BIG THICK ARMS!

9

10

215

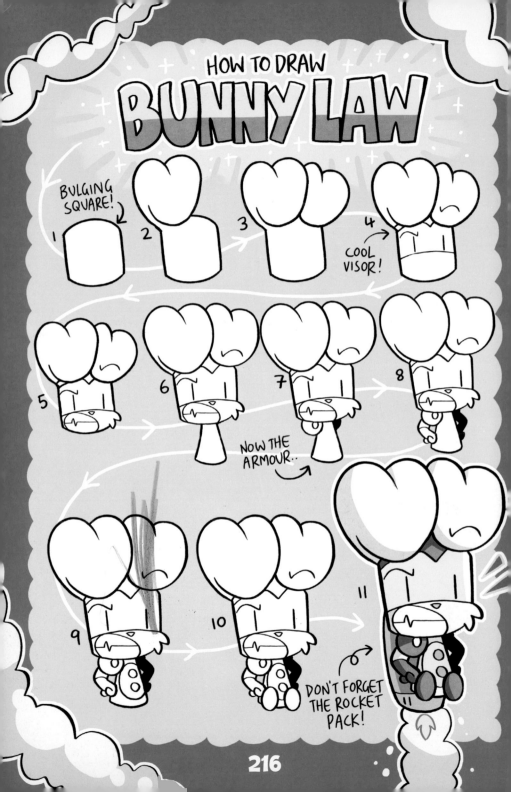

HOW TO DRAW
BUNNY LAW

BULGING SQUARE!

1

2

3

4 COOL VISOR!

5

6 NOW THE ARMOUR..

7

8

9

10

11 DON'T FORGET THE ROCKET PACK!

11

SPECIAL PREVIEW!

CLATTERS & BUMP — By James Turner

LOOK, BUMP, A FOX!

I'M AN UNLIVING HORROR THAT DEFIES THE VERY ORDER OF NATURE! WHY WOULD I CARE ABOUT A FOX?

I JUST THOUGHT YOU LIKED FOXES. WELL, I DON'T!

LATER... #1 FOX FAN FOXES

MEGA ROBO BROS — By Neill Cameron

UGH. I AM SO BORED. WHAT IS EVEN THE POINT OF ANYTHING?

"Life has no meaning a priori. It is up to you to give it a meaning, and value is nothing but the meaning that you choose."

FREDDY, WHAT ARE YOU DOING? I CHOOSE BISCUITS!

DONUT SQUAD — By Neill Cameron

EAT ME! EAT ME! OOH, DONUTS! DELICIOUS!

EAT ME! MMM, DON'T MIND IF I DO!

EAT ME! OH, NO THANKS! I'M ACTUALLY TRYING TO BE HEALTHY!

EAT ME, YOU COWARD!! MMPHGRGL!!!

DONUTS

Find brand-new SHORTS and hilarious comics in *The Phoenix*!

Wasn't that AWESOME?! This is just a tiny glimpse!

JAMIE SMART HAS BEEN CREATING CHILDREN'S COMICS FOR MANY YEARS, WITH POPULAR TITLES INCLUDING *BUNNY VS MONKEY, LOOSHKIN, MAX AND CHAFFY* FOR YOUNGER READERS, AND *FISH-HEAD STEVE,* WHICH BECAME THE FIRST WORK OF ITS KIND TO BE SHORTLISTED FOR THE ROALD DAHL FUNNY PRIZE.

THE FIRST FOUR BOOKS IN HIS *FLEMBER* SERIES OF ILLUSTRATED NOVELS ARE AVAILABLE NOW. HE ALSO WORKS ON MULTIMEDIA PROJECTS LIKE *FIND CHAFFY.*

JAMIE LIVES IN THE SOUTH-EAST OF ENGLAND, WHERE HE SPENDS HIS TIME THINKING UP STORIES AND GETTING LOST ON DOG WALKS.